The Bat Can Bat

A BOOK OF TRUE HOMONYMS

Gene Barretta

Christy Ottaviano Books

HENRY HOLT AND COMPANY
NEW YORK

A Note to the Reader

HOMONYMS are words that sound the same and are spelled the same but have different meanings, such as **BOWL** (a round dish) and **BOWL** (the sport).

HOMOPHONES are words that sound the same but are spelled differently and have different meanings, such as **TALE** (a story) and **TAIL** (a part of an animal).

HOMOGRAPHS are words that are spelled the same but pronounced differently and have different meanings, such as **TEAR** (to cry) and **TEAR** (to rip).

Henry Holt and Company, *Publishers since 1866*
Henry Holt® is a registered trademark of Macmillan Publishing Group, LLC
175 Fifth Avenue, New York, NY 10010 • mackids.com

Library of Congress Cataloging-in-Publication Data is available.
ISBN 978-0-8050-9946-1

Our books may be purchased in bulk for promotional, educational, or business use.
Please contact your local bookseller or the Macmillan Corporate and Premium Sales Department
at (800) 221-7945 ext. 5442 or by e-mail at MacmillanSpecialMarkets@macmillan.com.

First edition, 2018 / Designed by Patrick Collins
The artist used watercolor on Arches cold-press paper to create the illustrations for this book.
Printed in China by RR Donnelley Asia Printing Solutions Ltd., Dongguan City, Guangdong Province

10 9 8 7 6 5 4 3 2 1

For Christy Ottaviano,

This dedication to you is long, long overdue.

My editor my friend, a heartfelt thank you.

g.

The BAT can BAT! The fans rose to their FEET as the ball sailed over 400 FEET for a home run.

After the game, the president of the United STATES announced a groundbreaking law which STATES that every animal has the RIGHT to play sports.
"That's RIGHT!" he said. "Animals are athletes, too!"

The rabbits like to TRAIN for races
by racing a TRAIN down the TRACK.

They keep TRACK
of every hip and every hop.

The bulldog is TOUGH enough to BREAK
five boards without taking a BREAK.

The **TOUGH** part is keeping the slobber in his mouth.

Sound the HORN! Stop the game!
The water buffalo got his HORN
stuck in the net again.

The dolphin is an excellent surfer. She can STAND on top of a WAVE and WAVE at the judges' STAND.

Every golf CLUB at the golf CLUB
is too big for the poor little hamster.

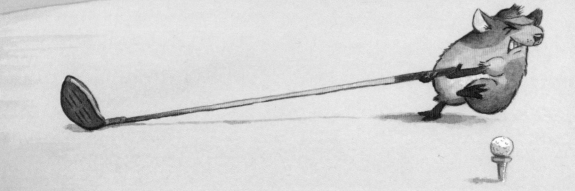

The **POINT** of fencing is to avoid the **POINT** of the sword.

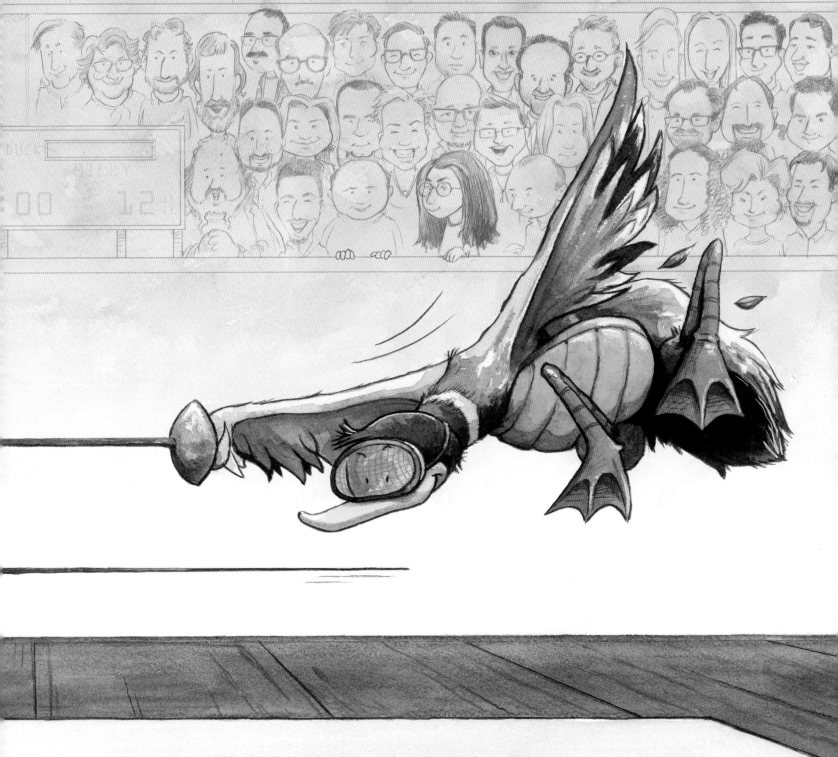

So, the FLY has to DUCK and the DUCK has to FLY.

The roller DERBY RAM is MEAN.
See what I MEAN?
He likes to RAM other players
with his pointy DERBY.

It's always a splashfest
when the turtles ROW
past the fans in the front ROW.

The **GOAL** of the ostrich
is to score a **GOAL**.

The AIM of the ostrich
is to AIM better.
Much, much better.

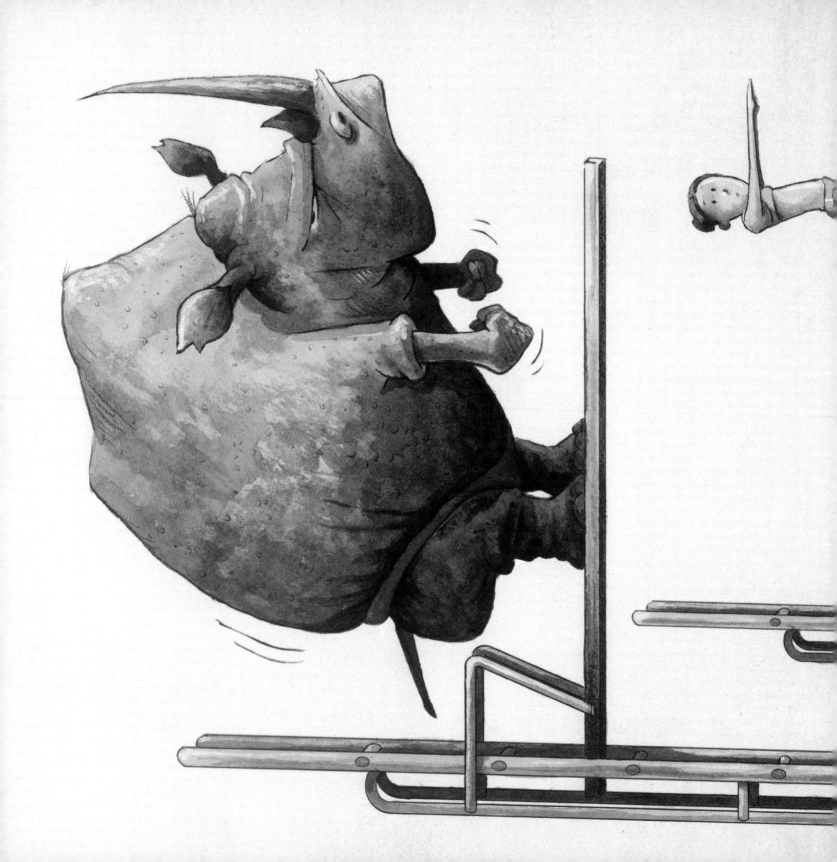

The rhino threw a FIT because his swimsuit didn't FIT.

When the STEER
tried to STEER his skateboard,
it didn't go very WELL.

He fell in a WELL.

The monkey has a BALL when he takes
his TURN playing quarterback.

He thinks it's funny to TURN around
and throw the BALL the wrong way.

The cougar makes an awful RACKET
when she swings her RACKET.

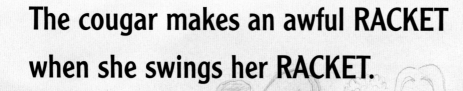

Still, it doesn't MATCH the noise
over at the elephant MATCH.

CRUNCH!

TOOOOOOT!

THUD!

The prickly, wrestling porcupine
was able to PIN his opponents
and win the championship.

Unfortunately, there is no PLACE
to PLACE his first PLACE PIN.

So, how do people feel about animal athletes?

"Me? I LIKE this new KIND of sport!"

“The president’s new law is great! It’s very KIND to animals.”

“I don’t. It’s LIKE an animal takeover!”

As a matter of fact, most people agree that animal athletes should be given the Presidential SEAL of Approval. And that's not surprising, since they also elected a SEAL for president!